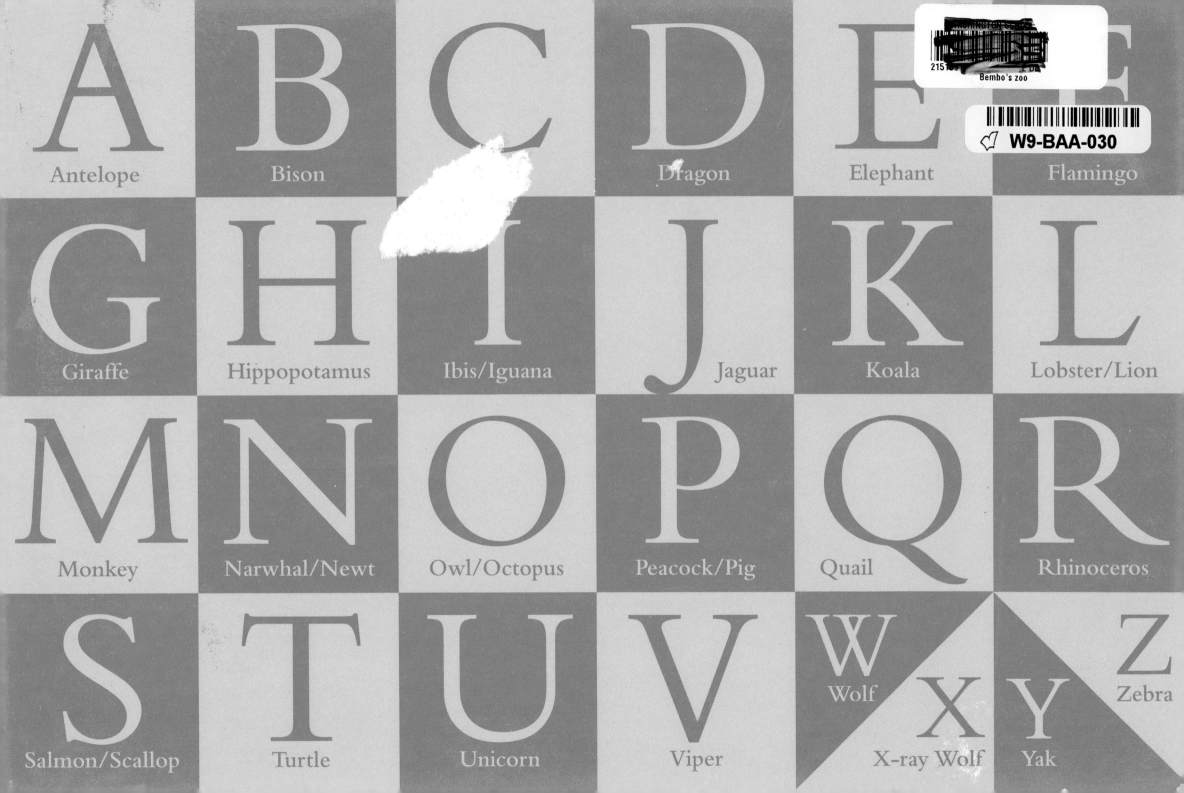

A Antelope
B Bison
C
D Dragon
E Elephant
F Flamingo

G Giraffe
H Hippopotamus
I/J Ibis/Iguana
J Jaguar
K Koala
L Lobster/Lion

M Monkey
N Narwhal/Newt
O Owl/Octopus
P Peacock/Pig
Q Quail
R Rhinoceros

S Salmon/Scallop
T Turtle
U Unicorn
V Viper
W Wolf
X X-ray Wolf
Y Yak
Z Zebra

Roberto de Vicq de Cumptich

Bembo's Zoo

HENRY HOLT AND COMPANY NEW YORK

AN ANIMAL ABC BOOK

Antelope

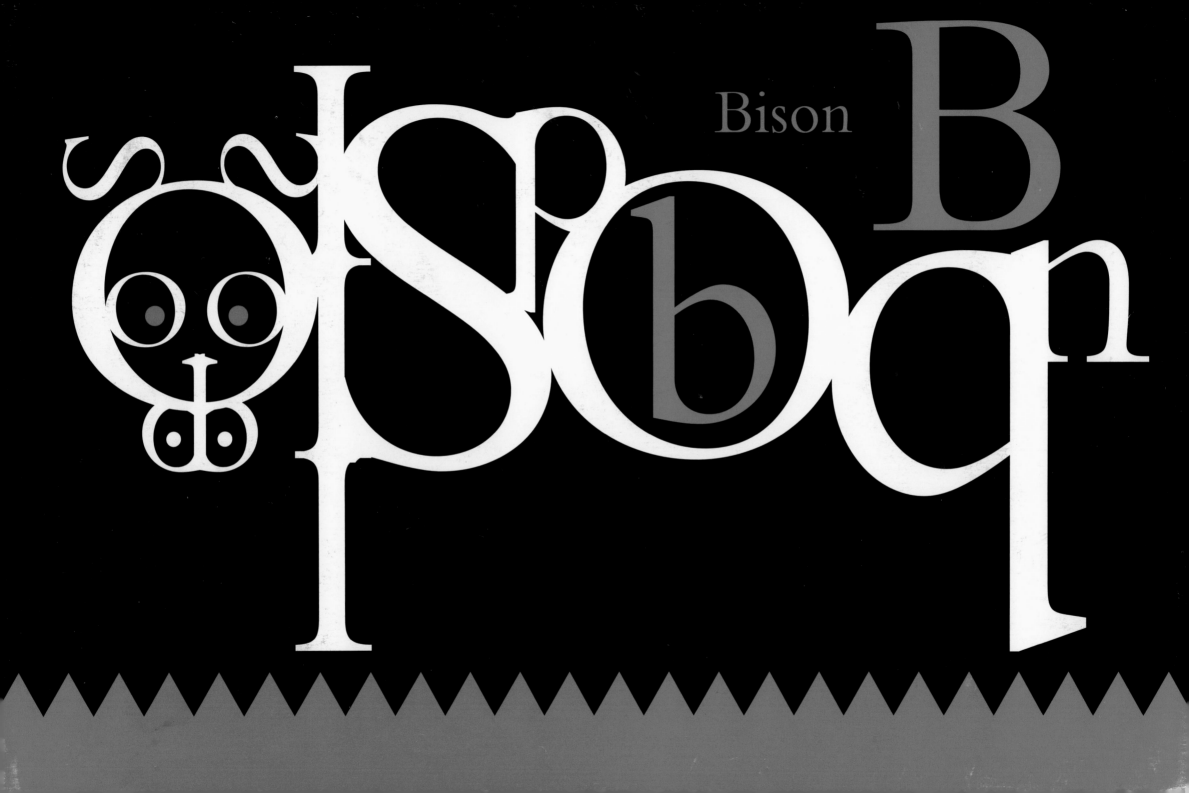

Bison

Crab

Dragon

Dd

Elephant

Flamingo

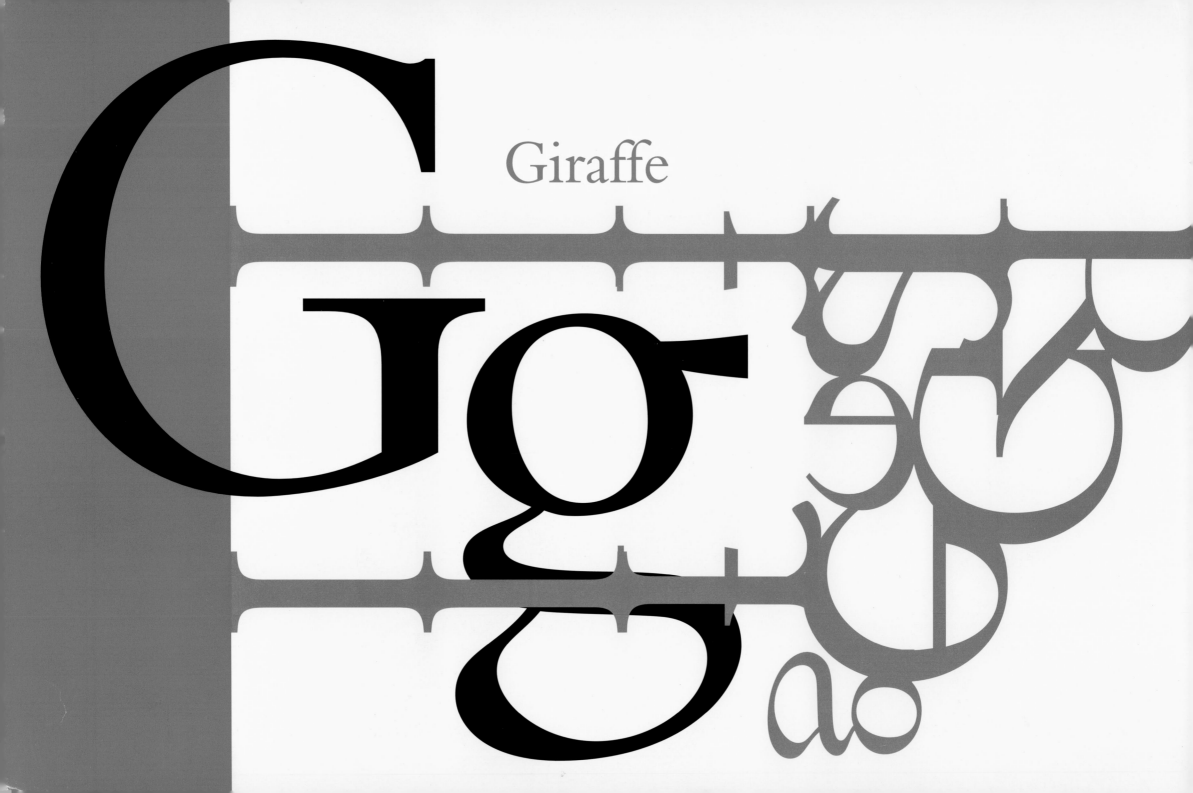

Giraffe

Hippopotamus

Ibis

Ii

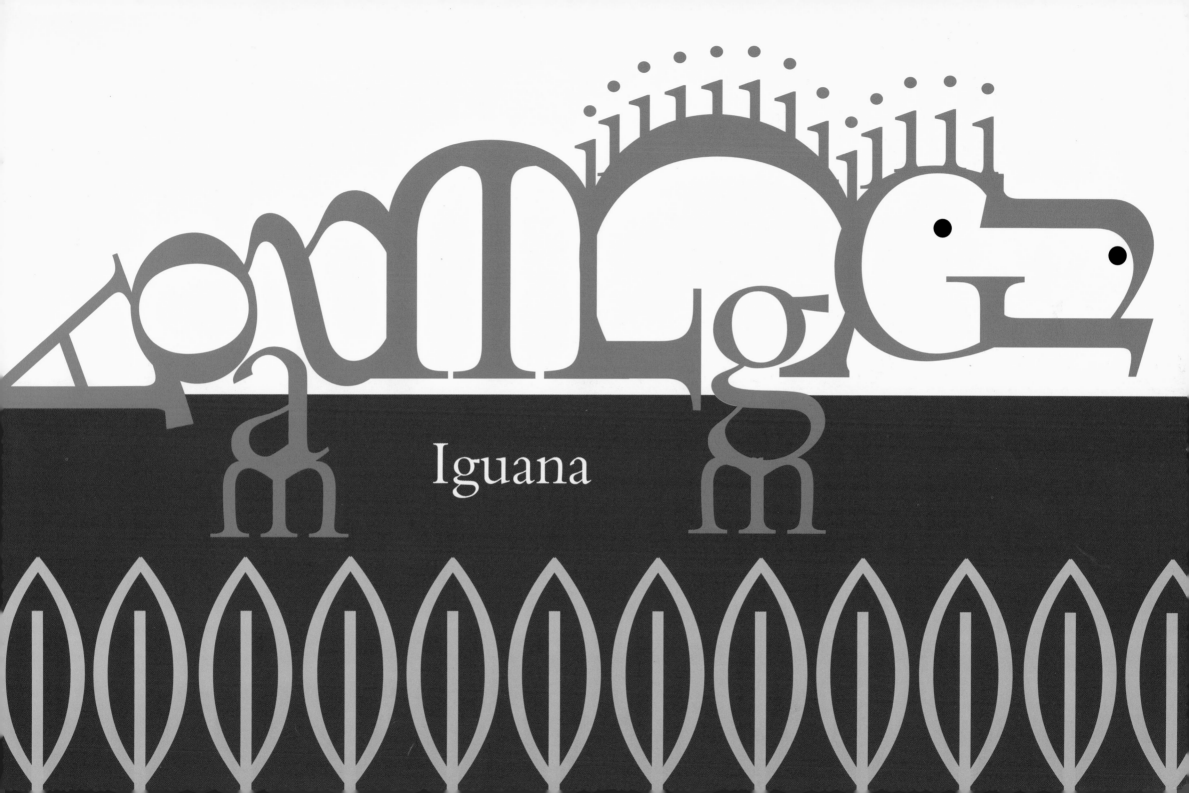

Iguana

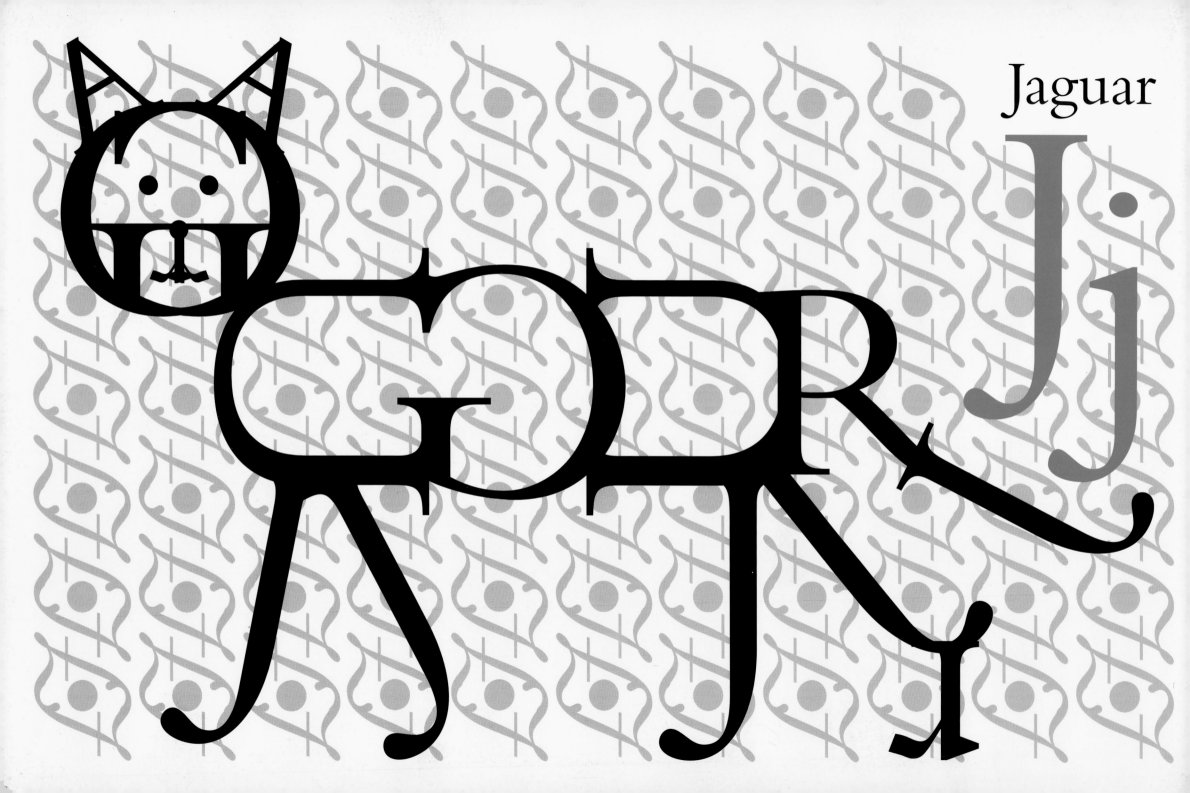

Jaguar

J j

Koala

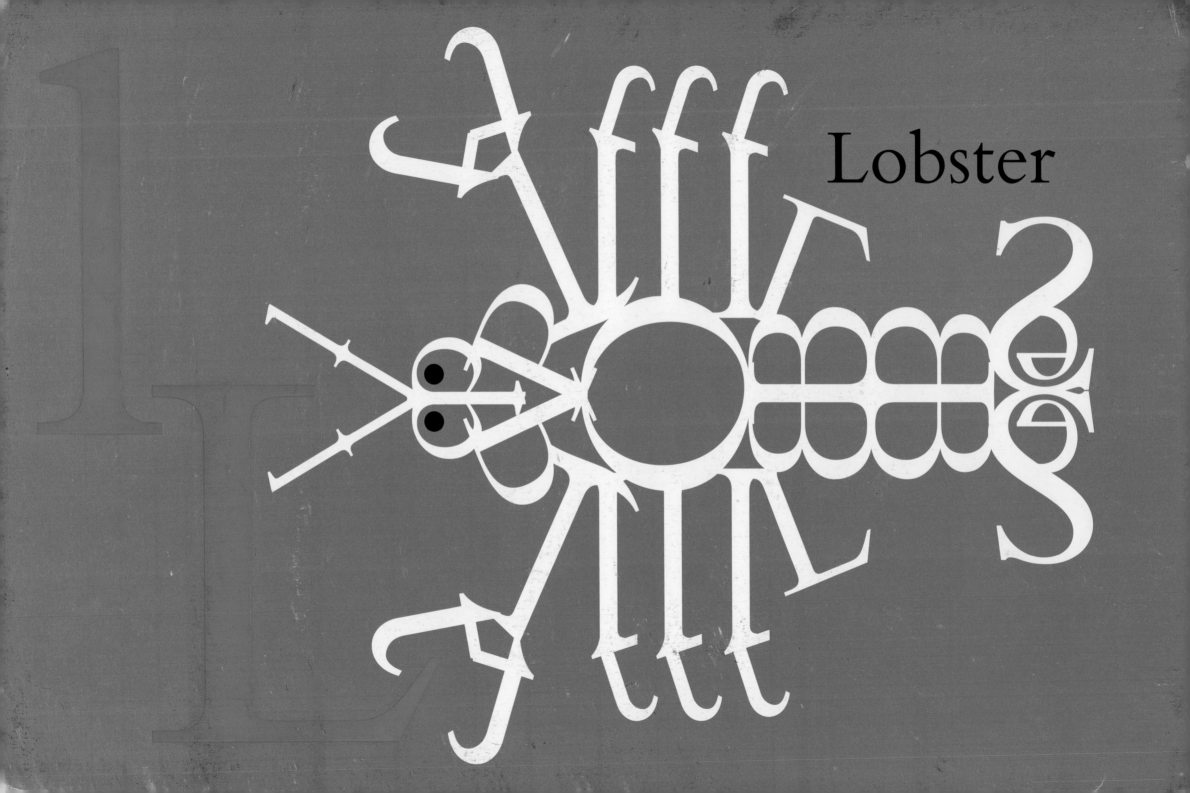

Lobster

Lion

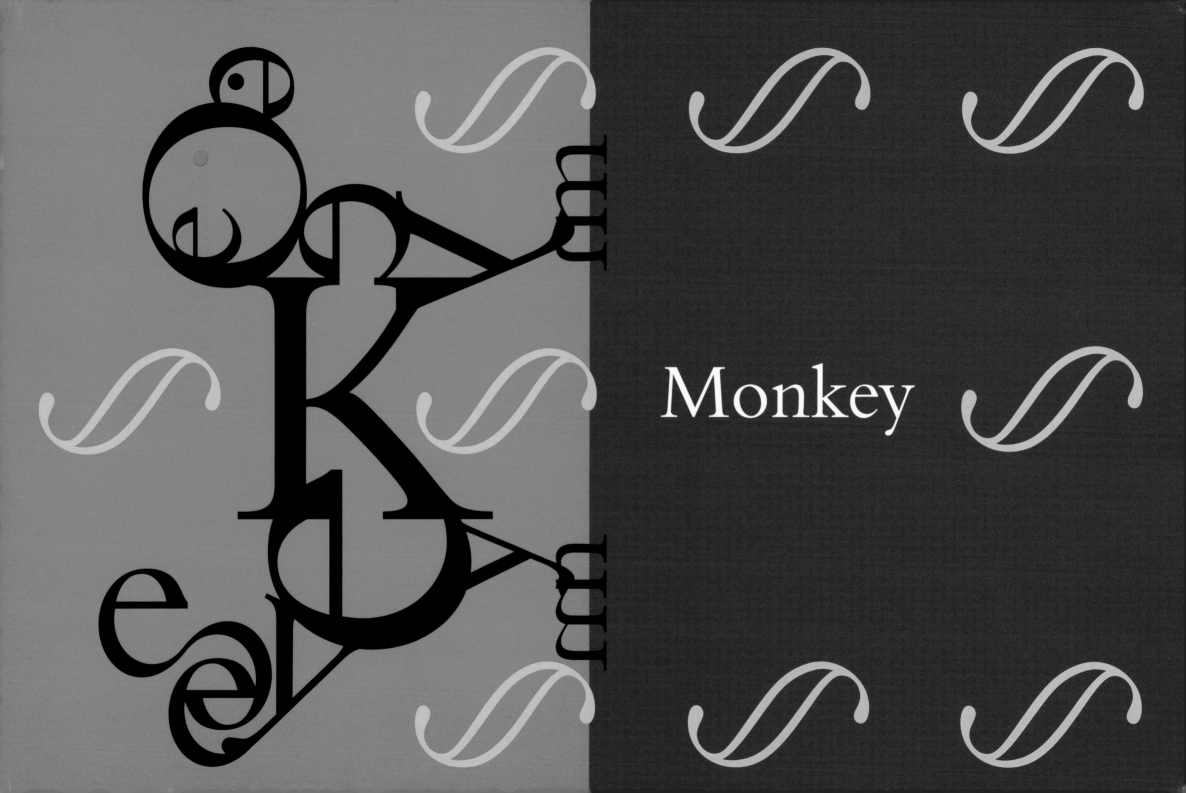

Monkey

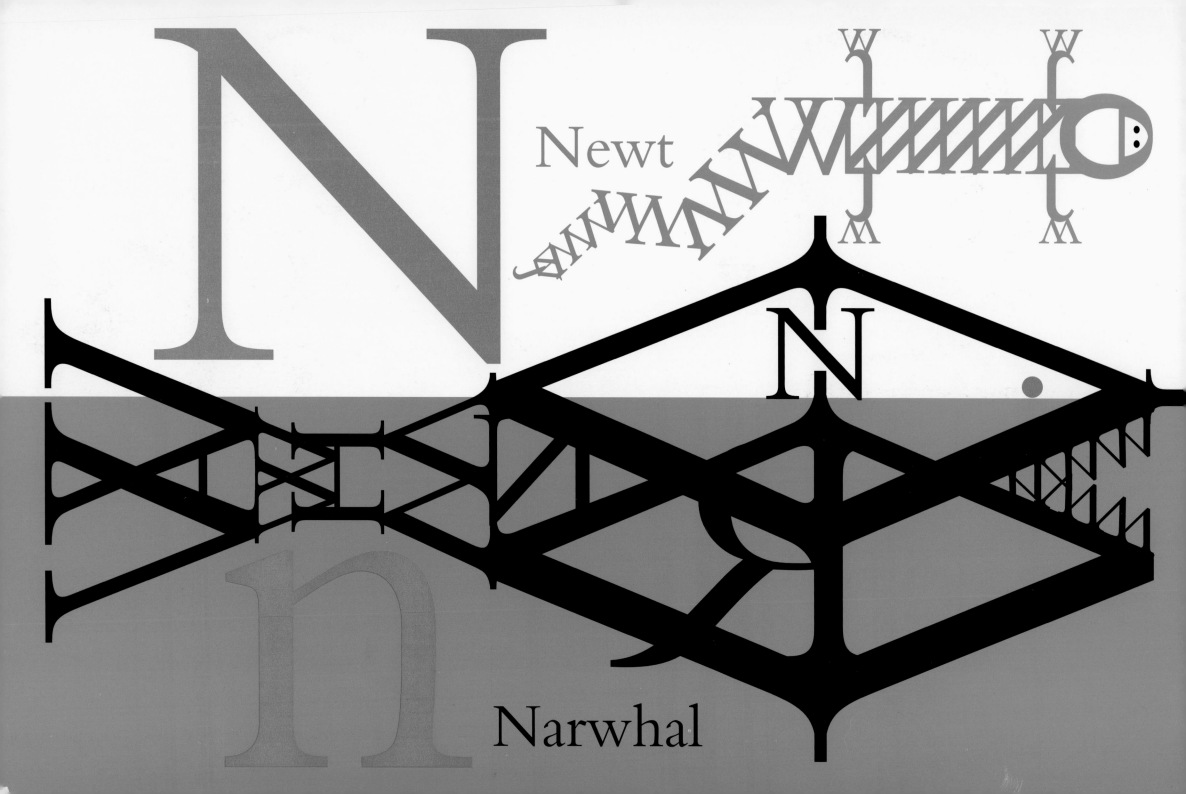

Newt

Narwhal

Owl

Octopus

Peacock

Pig

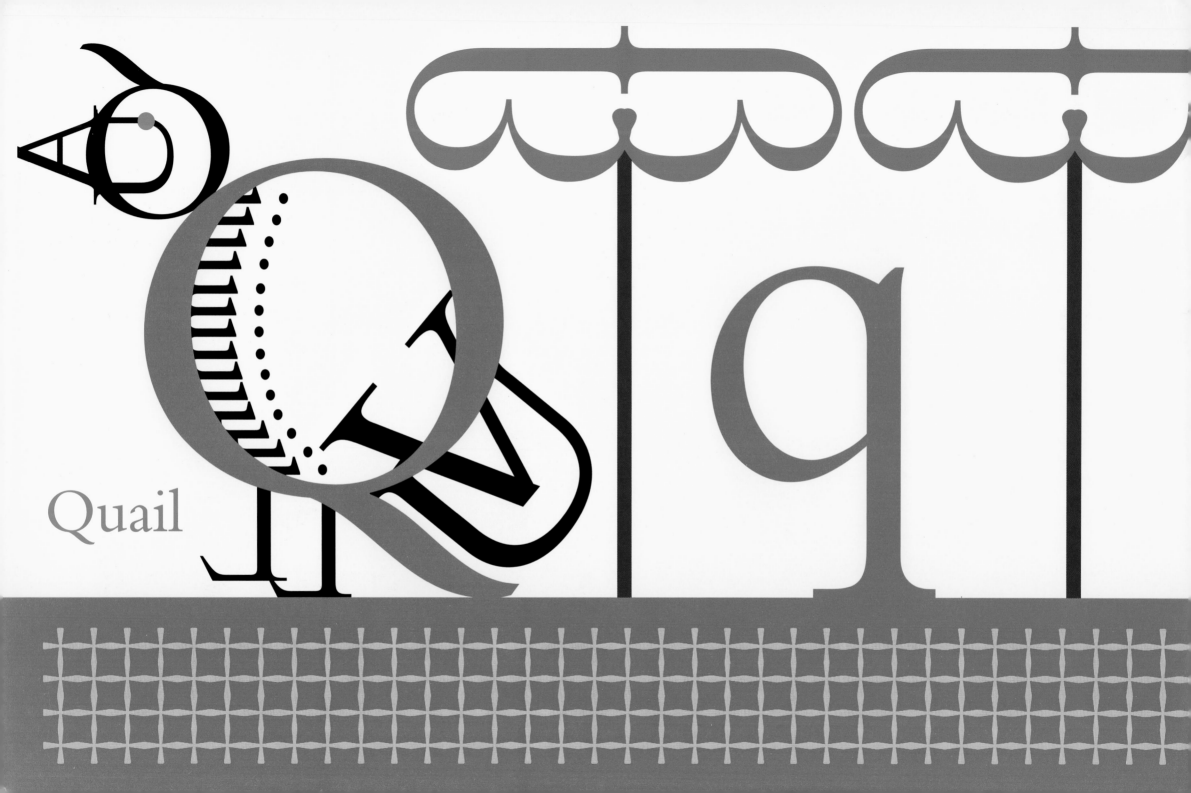

Quail

Rhinoceros

Salmon

Scallop

Turtle

tT

Unicorn

U U W

Viper

Wolf

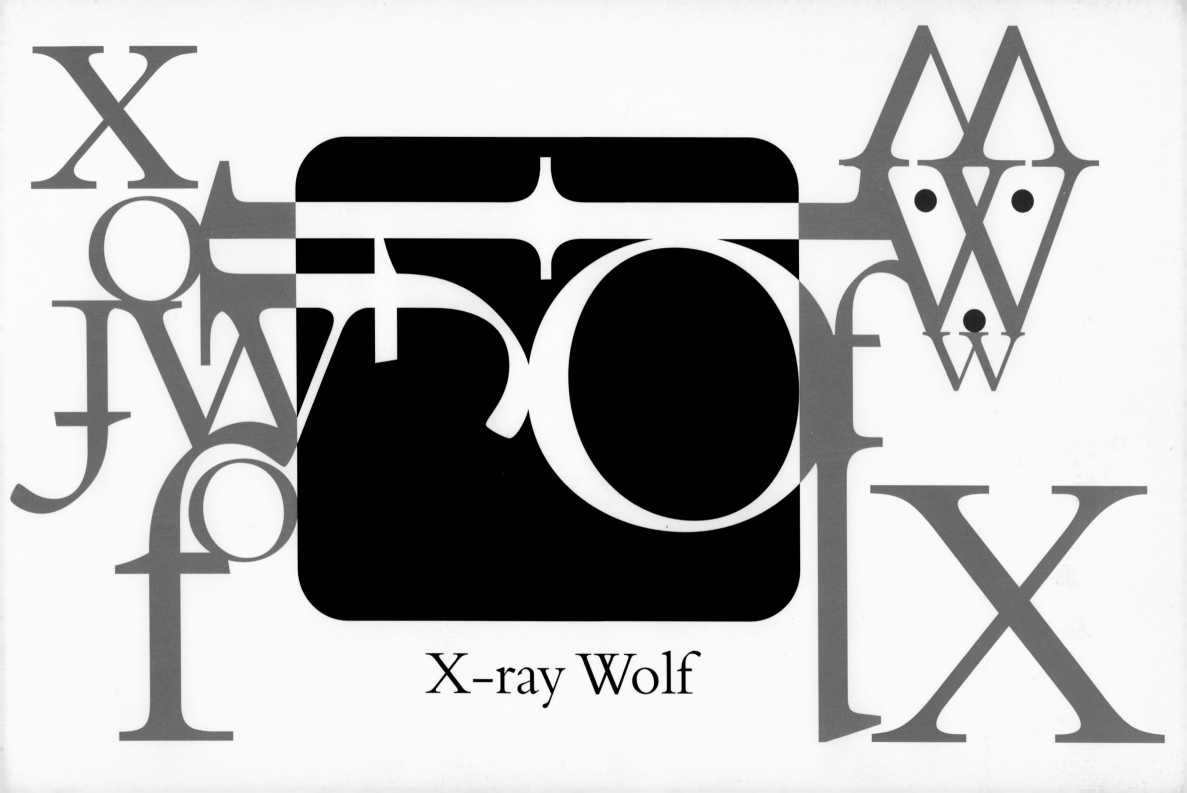

X-ray Wolf

Yak